This book
belongs to

Disney's
The Fox and the Hound

MOUSE WORKS

One early spring morning, Big Mama the owl, who
had been up all night hunting, was about to fall asleep
when something caught her eye. It was a she-fox
carrying a little cub in her mouth. The vixen quietly
went up to the fence of a nearby farm and gently put
her cub on the ground.

"Oh, my goodness! She left her cub behind!" cried
Big Mama as she watched the vixen run away. "Maybe
she wants to save her baby from the hunters I heard in
the forest last night. Poor little thing!"

3

Big Mama had a very kind heart. She flew down
from her branch to look at the cub. The tiny little ball
of fur was shaking with fear.

"Don't be afraid, little one," she whispered. "I'll
think of something!"

Big Mama was very wise. She would soon come up
with an idea.

Just then two shotgun blasts went off in the distance. The little fox started to whimper.

"Whoo, hoo-hoo, whoo, whoo!" called Big Mama urgently. Her friends Dinky the sparrow and Boomer the woodpecker flew over to the fence.

"Who is this?" asked Boomer, pointing at the little fox.

"Why isn't he with his parents?" asked Dinky. Big Mama quickly explained what she had seen.

"Did you hear those shots just now? This little fox is an orphan and we have to find him a home before something happens to him."

"Who lives in that farm over there?" asked Big Mama, who had an idea.

"A very kind elderly widow," said Dinky. "Her name is Mrs. Tweed and she always feeds me in the winter."

"But will she want a baby fox?" objected Boomer. "How will we bring him to her anyhow?"

"Do you see that laundry drying in the sun? I am sure Mrs. Tweed would come down to this end of the field to pick something up if it had blown away..." said Big Mama. "Follow me!"

The three birds flew over to the laundry line and picked some linen off it.

They flew back and wrapped the cub in the linen. Then they went to a nearby tree and waited.

Mrs. Tweed soon came out of the house to get her laundry. She was a little surprised that her tablecloth had blown away because there was no wind that morning. She went to pick it up, as Big Mama had said she would, and gasped when a tiny ball of red fur rolled out onto the field.

"Oh! A little baby fox!" she cried as she picked up the frightened animal. "Have you been abandoned? I'll take care of you."

She carried the cub into the house while Big Mama Dinky, and Boomer looked on, pleased that their plan had worked.

Inside the house, Mrs. Tweed prepared a bottle of milk and, holding the cub like a baby, she fed him.

"Since you found your way into my field and my tablecloth, I shall keep you!" decided the kind old lady. "Your name will be Tod."

With that, she gave her new friend a hug.

Across from Mrs. Tweed's farm lived a hunter named Amos Slade. The day Mrs. Tweed found Tod, Amos Slade brought back a little surprise for his old hound Chief.

"Here is a friend and student for you," said Amos, handing him a mysterious bag. "I trust you will take care of him and teach him how to hunt. His name is Copper."

Copper was an adorable little puppy. "What am I going to do with a puppy?" growled the grumpy Chief.

Chief was a courageous hunting hound. He had
hunted for Amos Slade for many years and he was
very proud of the many hares, quails, pheasants, and
foxes he had helped his master catch. Chief felt
important. What would a silly little puppy like Copper
amount to?

"You'd better obey me," growled Chief, looking
mean. The little puppy licked the big dog on the nose.

"Well, as long as you obey me," added Chief,
softening up, "everything should work out."

Copper had already won the big old hound's heart.

Time went by. Tod grew a little stronger and a little bigger every day and so did Copper. One morning, when he could not find Big Mama, Dinky, and Boomer to play with, Tod ventured out of the farm into the woods.

He was busy sniffing all the exciting new scents
when all of a sudden he ran into Copper, who was also
out sniffing.

"Oh, great! Someone to play with!" thought Tod,
and he politely said hello.

"He's a funny-looking dog," thought Copper, "but he
looks friendly." So he said hello back. Soon the fox
and the hound were very good friends.

They romped through the woods, chased each other down paths and jumped into a pond together. *Splash!* They could not stop laughing. When it was time to go home, they vowed to spend every day together.

Every day they met and played in the woods. But
one morning, Copper was not there. Tod decided to go
look for him at Amos's house. He found his friend tied
to a doghouse made from a barrel. He was very
surprised. Mrs. Tweed never tied *him* up.

Tod was even more surprised to find another dog, a
lot bigger than Copper, sleeping in a second barrel and
also tied up.

"Is this Chief?" he asked his friend, who had told
him about his older companion.

"He must be a very kind daddy," Tod added, a little
envious. He stepped up to Chief and gave him a
friendly hug. But the old hound, recognizing the scent
of his enemy the fox, woke up growling. Tod stepped
back, confused. Why wouldn't Chief like him?

Before Copper could warn his friend, Chief leapt towards Tod. The frightened little fox ran away but Chief, furious, chased him through the yard dragging his barrel with him and barking madly. The hens clucked and fluttered in all directions as Tod wove his way through them. What a racket! Amos came out of his house with his gun. He fired a shot, thinking that Tod wanted to steal one of his chickens. But the little fox was running away as fast as he could.

Tod leapt over the fence and tore up the road, just as Mrs. Tweed drove by, taking her milk to sell at the market. He jumped into the back of her truck and hid in between the milk containers.

When Mrs. Tweed and Tod returned from the market, an angry Amos was waiting for them at the door.

"I don't want your wicked fox near my hens, do you understand!" he shouted at Mrs. Tweed. "Next time I'll shoot him!"

"Don't you dare shoot my fox, Mr. Slade! He's a well-behaved pet and he wouldn't go near your chickens! I'll bet you scared him," she replied firmly. "Now get off my property!" she ordered.

Mrs. Tweed did not know what had happened to Tod, but she could tell from his frightened, innocent look that he had not done anything wrong.

"Amos meant what he said, though," thought the old lady. "I'd better keep Tod inside the house or that mean hunter may hurt him!"

So she kept Tod inside the house with her and took him out for walks every day.

Tod was soon very bored. He missed the fresh air and the fun he always had with Big Mama, Dinky, and Boomer. He also missed Copper and often wondered how his friend was.

One morning, Tod said to himself, "I am bigger and stronger. Nothing will happen to me! I'll sneak out of the house and see Copper."

He went from window to window until he found one ajar. He squeezed out through the opening and headed straight through the woods to Amos's house.

"What a wonderful morning!" he sang, skipping up
the path. "I can't wait to see Copper. Maybe we can
play together," he thought happily.

He had not forgotten about the mean Chief, so when
he got to Copper's house, he carefully looked around
for his friend. But there was no one there.

Tod then heard a loud bang and an engine start. There were Amos, Chief, and Copper in the car driving away. Chief sat proudly in the front seat by his master, but Copper did not seem pleased in the back.

"Chief! Explain to that lazy dog that we are going to teach him to hunt," shouted the hunter.

Chief growled in Copper's direction.

Tod watched them leave. They were going to hunt, but what did that mean? Were they going to chase some poor animal who had not hurt them?

"Copper would never do that," thought Tod. "He is a good dog."

He was sad to see his friend go. He ran over to Big Mama and explained to her what he had seen.

"What will happen to Copper?" he asked her.

"Copper will be just fine," she told him. "He will learn to track for Amos. Amos is a hunter. During the hunting season, he catches animals for food and for their furs. Copper will help him find the animals."

"But that's awful, Big Mama!" said Tod as a shiver went down his spine.

"Don't worry, Tod, you will be all right with Mrs. Tweed," said the owl reassuringly, and she gave him a hug.

Days flew by and winter came. Tod was lonely and
missed his friend Copper very much. Every day, he
looked out the window hoping to see him. Then one
day he saw big white feathers falling from the sky.

"That's snow," explained Mrs. Tweed. Soon a white
mantle covered the countryside.

It was cold outside. Dinky and Boomer huddled under the scarecrow's hat, which no longer frightened them. Big Mama was sleeping in a tree trunk. Everything was very quiet.

"Tod is lucky," said Dinky to Boomer. "He must be so warm inside!"

"Brrrrr, it's cold out here," agreed the woodpecker.

Meanwhile, high up in the mountains, Copper was learning how to track under Chief's supervision. He had grown a lot and was as big as Chief. He felt the urge to hunt and had learned to recognize all different kinds of scents. Chief was very proud of his student's progress, and Amos was pleased as well.

"Copper will make a wonderful hound. The next hunting season will be very good!" Amos told himself.

Winter slowly gave way to spring and the leaves grew back on the trees tender and green. Flowers sprang up in the fields and birds chirped in the countryside.

Tod had also grown a lot through the winter and he had become a very handsome fox. The first day Mrs. Tweed let him out, he ran to his friends Big Mama, Dinky, and Boomer.

"How tall you are!" squeaked Dinky.

"And how good-looking, too!" added Boomer.

"And to think he was only a little ball of fur a few months ago!" said Big Mama proudly.

All of a sudden, a loud rumbling noise broke the
country silence. Tod ran to see Amos, Chief, and
Copper driving up the road. This time Copper sat in
the front next to his master and Chief was in the back.

"Copper is back!" cried Tod with joy. "I'll go see
him tonight!"

"Watch out, Tod. Copper is a grown hound now.
He's learned how to hunt," warned Big Mama.

"Don't worry, Big Mama. I'll be very careful,"
replied Tod confidently. "I'll wait until Chief is sound
asleep to see Copper !"

That night, after Mrs. Tweed had gone to bed, Tod
slipped out of the house. He ran over to Amos's house.
Copper immediately recognized his old friend, but he
was not happy to see him.

"You have to go, Tod! I am a hound now and I hunt
foxes. You are not safe here," he warned the fox.

"But I'm not just any fox, Copper! I'm your friend!"
protested Tod.

"I'm sorry, but I can't be your friend anymore. I can't help it. I was born to hunt your kind. That's the way it is," said the hound firmly.

Tod was very disappointed. He could not understand why Copper did not want to be his friend anymore.

A howl stopped him short in his thoughts. Chief had awakened, smelling the fox. The old hound started to bark, pulling at his chain to free himself. Tod leapt away and started to run. He remembered only too well how Chief had chased him once before.

Then three gunshots went off in the night. Tod panicked. Amos would shoot him if he saw him. All of a sudden he remembered how angry the hunter had been at him. The fox zigzagged through the field, running as fast as he could.

Tod was so afraid that he lost his way. He climbed a little hill and skidded down a slope. Quickly he slipped underneath a pile of lumber next to some railroad tracks. He was panting and shaking with fear when Copper came up to him.

"Amos and Chief are coming after you. Run that way!" said the hound, pointing up the tracks to a bridge. "I've led them the other way. I don't want them to find you. Good luck!"

With that, Copper left. Tod was happy that Copper was his friend after all. He ran up the railroad tracks as his friend had told him with lightness in his heart.

But a nasty surprise awaited him at the bridge. Chief
had not been fooled by Copper's diversion. When he
saw Tod, the hound started to bark triumphantly.

All of a sudden a thundering sound shook the bridge.
A train was coming at high speed. Tod instinctively
flattened himself between the rails but Chief was not so
lucky. He desperately tried to jump to the side, but fell
off the bridge into the ravine below.

Tod was terrified as the train passed over him. But the train went by and he was not hurt. The fox slowly made his way to Mrs. Tweed's farm, hoping that Chief would be all right.

On the way home, he thought, "Big Mama was right. This is a dangerous world for a fox to live in. But she was wrong about Copper. He is my friend after all!"

The thought cheered him up. But Copper, who had found Chief in the ravine, was filled with anger and confusion. As he licked his friend's wounds, waiting for Amos to fetch them, he started to blame Tod for the accident.

"I will avenge you," he told Chief. "I won't allow Tod ever to hurt you like this again. He's a fox! And I hunt foxes. They're *not* my friends. Why did I ever let him get away?"

When Tod came back into the house, he slipped into his foster mother's arms for comfort.

She soon found out where Tod had been. Someone
was banging on the front door. It was Amos, and he
was very mad.

"Your stupid fox almost got my hound killed!" he
screamed, shaking his fist. "You have no right keeping a
mean and wild animal in your home."

"Mr. Slade, *you* are mean and wild. Leave my fox
alone!" shouted back Mrs. Tweed. "Good night!"

The hunter walked away, swearing revenge.

Mrs. Tweed was disturbed by what Amos had said. "I am sure Tod wouldn't hurt a soul," she thought. "But Tod is a fox and foxes are supposed to live in the woods, not on farms. I can't keep him inside the house all the time; he needs to roam in the forest! That's in his nature. What should I do?"

Mrs. Tweed wanted two things. She wanted Tod to stay alive and she wanted him to be happy. She decided to take him to a wildlife sanctuary nearby. No one was allowed to hurt animals there, and Amos would have to leave Tod alone.

The next morning, she brought her little friend there, took off his collar and said good-bye.

"Now be good," she told him. "I hope you make a lot of friends in the woods. And don't be sad! You'll be very happy here."

After Mrs. Tweed had gone, Tod felt very sad. He couldn't understand why he had been taken away from his friends and his home.

"What will I do now?" he thought sadly as he walked into the strange forest.

Amos Slade watched Mrs. Tweed come back from the
wildlife sanctuary alone. He could not see Tod
anywhere. Slyly, he went up to the farm.

"Where is Tod?" he asked the old lady.

"Tod won't bother you any more, Mr. Slade. I've
taken him to the wildlife sanctuary," she replied,
unhappily.

Amos ran back home. "That wicked fox won't get
away!" he thought. "I can't hunt in the sanctuary, but
I've got an idea."

He took out some tools and made a trap as Copper
looked on.

"We'll catch that fox with this, Copper!" he told his
hound. "He'll step into this and *snap*! It'll close on his
leg. Wait till Chief sees this!"

The old hound was resting with his hurt leg in a
bandage.

Copper snarled his approval.

51

Meanwhile, in the wildlife sanctuary, Big Mama was
very busy looking for Tod. The owl had found out
what had happened from Dinky and Boomer and she
was very worried. What would happen to Tod? He did
not know how to survive in the forest because he had
always lived on the farm.

She looked and looked but could not find him. Then she ran into a beautiful she-fox. Her name was Vixey.

"Have you seen a handsome and kind fox around?" Big Mama asked her.

"No, I haven't," replied Vixey. "But I'll help you find him, if you'd like."

So Big Mama and Vixey set out to find Tod.

Tod was not very far away. He had spent the night curled up in the curve of a branch, as he had seen Big Mama do. But it wasn't very comfortable and he had not slept very well. He was having miserable thoughts. When he turned around to get more comfortable, he slipped off the branch...

...and landed right on top of a badger who was coming out of his burrow.

"Ouch! Go home!" snarled the badger.

"I wish I could, but I don't have a home any more," said Tod politely.

"Well, you can't stay with me!" snorted the unfriendly animal.

Tod sadly walked away, longing for his friends.

"Where will I go now?" he thought. "There must be a place for me to live. How I wish I were back at the farm!"

He followed a path through the woods, dragging his tail on the ground. It was Big Mama who saw him first.

"Look, Vixey! There he is!" cried the owl, relieved.
Vixey let out a gasp. She had not expected Tod to be
so handsome.

Tod heard her cry and turned around, hoping to see
a friendly face. When he saw the lovely she-fox, his
face lit up.

"Wow!" he thought. "How beautiful she is!"

Then he saw Big Mama. What a surprise!

"Big Mama! Is that really you?" he cried.

The owl gave him a big hug. "I am so happy
to have found you," she said. "This is Vixey.
I hope you can become good friends."

Tod blushed. He had already fallen in love.

Vixey could tell that Tod was very hungry. She volunteered to take him to a stream and teach him how to fish.

Big Mama called "Whoo, hoo-hoo, whoo, whoo" for Dinky and Boomer, who had also been looking for Tod. They came flying and congratulated Big Mama on finding their friend. The owl introduced them to Vixey.

"Isn't she beautiful!" whispered Dinky to Boomer.
"Yes, she is, and Tod seems to think so, too,"
giggled Boomer as he watched the two foxes fishing.
"What a handsome couple they make!" he added.

By the afternoon, Amos was ready to catch Tod.
He had made three traps. He used pliers to cut open
the barbed wire that surrounded the wildlife
sanctuary, snickering with anticipation. Copper was
with him, and he ordered his hound to find Tod's track.

Copper put his nose to the ground. Within minutes,
he had found Tod's scent. The track led him to a tree.
Amos laid the traps on the path by the tree and
covered them with leaves.

"Good work, Copper!" he congratulated his hound.
"If that fox has been here once before, he'll be back!
Let's wait for him."

The hunter and the hound settled behind a hillock. A short time went by and they heard some noise. Amos and Copper looked over the hump. Tod and Vixey were further up the path, sitting side by side.

They were saying good-bye to each other. Big Mama, Dinky, and Boomer had left earlier so that the two foxes could be alone.

"Can I see you tomorrow?" asked Tod shyly.

Vixey nodded yes. She was very happy.

Tod kissed Vixey good-bye and strolled back to his tree. A shiny object in the grass caught his eye. He pushed a pebble at it. The steel jaws of one of Amos's traps snapped shut. Tod jumped back in fear. At that moment, Amos stood up. He was furious that Tod had outwitted him. He raised his gun to shoot, but Tod ran back up the path after Vixey, setting off Amos's other two traps.

Tod soon caught up with Vixey and quickly
explained to her what had happened.

"Follow me! I'll take you to my burrow. We'll be
safe there," she said and started to run. Tod followed
her through the woods and slipped into the opening to
her burrow after her. But Amos had sent Copper after
them, and the hound saw them disappear into the
ground.

Tod had never been in a burrow before. "This is big,"
he said to Vixey.

"I hope to raise a family here one day," she
explained shyly.

Tod blushed. Maybe they would have a family
together. He forgot about Amos and Copper and said,
"That would be wonderful!"

Just then a strange smell crept into the burrow.

"What's that smell?" asked Tod. "It sort of smells
like Mrs. Tweed's kitchen."

"Smoke!" cried Vixey in alarm. "It's smoke! They found us!"

Tod did not understand.

"When a hunter finds a burrow," explained Vixey quickly, "he lights a fire at one opening. He knows the smoke will drive us out of the burrow through the back exit, or we will die. We're trapped! Our only chance is to jump through the fire because Amos will be waiting for us at the other exit."

Tod and Vixey courageously jumped out of the burrow through the fire. Vixey was right. Amos was waiting at the other exit, which Copper had found.

The two foxes ran up the mountainside along a river to the safety of the woods. But Copper spotted them and Amos, more than ever determined to get them, ordered his hound to chase them.

Copper led the chase,
barking madly. He put
everything into keeping up
with the foxes and Amos
followed, proud of his
hound's determination.

Tod and Vixey ran for their lives and plunged ahead, jumping over rocks and weaving through the trees. Tod could not understand why his old friend was chasing after them. What would happen to them?

Luck was on their side. They leapt across the river
from stone to stone and darted through a meadow.
Copper and Amos soon followed, but they ran straight
into a huge grizzly bear who was foraging in the field.
The bear had not seen many humans before and was
angry at the intrusion. With a great roar, he raised
himself on his hind legs and towered over the hunter.

Amos dropped his gun and let out a scream of panic. Bears are dangerous when they have been disturbed, and Amos was afraid. As he started to run away he stepped into an old trap, long forgotten, on the ground. The trap closed on his foot with a loud snap. Amos screamed with pain and fell to the ground.

The bear started to move closer, furious that the intruders were not leaving his territory. Amos desperately tried to get the trap off his foot. Copper bravely stood between his master and the wild animal, barking and growling. But the bear was not afraid. When Copper attacked, he swept the dog off the ground with his huge paw. Amos screamed again hoping to scare the bear away, but the grizzly, satisfied that the hound lay unconscious, turned towards the hunter again.

When Tod heard Copper's barking and Amos's screams, he stopped.

"Vixey, listen! I think something awful is happening to Copper and Amos," he said, alarmed. "I must go back and find out."

Vixey was surprised. "How can you be so concerned with them after they tried to kill us? We're lucky to be alive. I think we must get as far away as we can."

"I can't, Vixey. You go ahead. I can't abandon Copper. He was my friend," said Tod, and he headed back to the meadow.

"Be careful!" called Vixey after him.

When Tod reached the meadow, he was horrified. An animal ten times larger than Copper loomed over his friend. Copper was trying to get back on his feet but he was still stunned by the bear's blow. Amos lay on the ground in pain.

Tod watched the huge beast move heavily towards his friend and quickly thought, "The only way I can help is if I take advantage of my speed and size."

Tod darted in front of the bear who then stopped
short, trying to figure out what had crossed his path.
The fox spun around and jumped on the animal's back
and bit his ear. The bear roared, but before he could
shake off his attacker, Tod was nipping at his ankles.
Amos couldn't believe his eyes.

The bear was raving mad now and when he saw the
little red fox ahead, he took off after him. Tod led him
away from Copper and Amos towards the river.

At the river, Tod stepped onto an old tree trunk reaching over the turbulent rapids. The bear followed him out over the water, convinced he had cornered his prey. But the trunk, rotted by age and the water, gave way with a terrifying crack. Both the bear and the fox plunged into the torrent below. The bear crashed into the water with a bellow and fell silent. Tod swam to the bank and hoisted himself onto the ground. He was exhausted.

When he looked up,
Amos loomed over him,
with his shotgun aimed at
him. Tod stared back in
disbelief. He had saved the
hunter's life! Would Amos
shoot him after all? The fox
was too exhausted to run.
He sat still, resigned to his
fate.

Just as Amos was about to fire, Copper jumped in front of his friend. He was grateful that Tod had so courageously saved their lives.

"If Amos shoots you, he will have to shoot me, too," said the hound to his friend.

Copper looked up at his master and let out a little bark.

Amos was confused. He thought a minute, then lowered his gun, and said, "Copper, you're right. Your friend should go free. Thanks for saving us, little fox."

With that, he turned and walked away. The animals breathed a sigh of relief. Tod followed Copper to the edge of the forest. He was happy that they were friends again.

"Good-bye, Copper," he said. "I must run and go find Vixey!"

"Good-bye, Tod, and thank you!" called the hound after him.

When Amos left the sanctuary, he headed straight to Mrs. Tweed's farm. She was very surprised to see him.

"You were right, Mrs. Tweed," he told her. "Your fox is awful nice."

He explained to her everything that Tod had done. The old lady beamed with pride. She was happy to know that Tod was safe.

"Shall I take care of your foot?" she volunteered.

Amos was delighted. He was beginning to like the widow, after all.

Amos and Mrs. Tweed became very good friends. Chief's wounds healed with time and the old hound forgave Tod after he heard that the fox had saved his master's and Copper's lives.

"And I thought all foxes were bad!" he would say, in disbelief.

Copper often thought of his brave friend and wondered how he fared in the woods.

Tod and Vixey were very
happy together. They often
sat on the cliff overlooking
the valley and wished their
friends below much
happiness.

"Do you know what the
two most beautiful things in
the world are?" Tod once
told Vixey. "Love and
friendship."

She agreed.

And they lived happily
ever after.

Published by Mouse Works, an imprint of Penguin Books USA Inc., 375 Hudson Street, New York, New York 10014
© 1993 The Walt Disney Company. All rights reserved. No part of this publication may be reproduced, stored in a
retrieval system, or transmitted in any form, by any means, electronic, mechanical, photocopying or otherwise,
without first obtaining written permission of the copyright owners.
Mouse Works™ is a trademark of The Walt Disney Company.
Printed in the United States of America.

ISBN 0-453-03035-1

10 9 8 7 6 5 4 3